Layout and design by Gary B Lewis

Lewis, Gary B, 1952—

He took my lunch: *a miracle through the eyes of a boy*

1. Christian—Fiction. 2. Faith—Personal I. Title.

ISBN: 978-0-6455552-4-0

PUBLISHED BY GARY B LEWIS

Cranbourne East, VICTORIA 3977

gazzablew@bigpond.com

He took my lunch!

A miracle through the eyes of a boy

One of several incredibly crafted backstories

in a series of miraculous events

* (story of feeding the five thousand)

TRIBUTES

During our lives we will all have had many tutors and mentors in various areas of expertise. Some may have simply been passing through and yet, in the intersection of time, places and personalities, something transpired. Looking back, it was enough to leave a lasting impression.

I'm also sure that, just like me, there have been some mentors you have not even met… like authors, presenters and preachers. Writers such as Max Lucado and Philip Yancey. Presenters such as Zig Ziglar and Nick Vujicic. Preachers like Chuck Swindoll and Robert Schuller. And, of course, others who would have journeyed with you for many years.

I recall one of those 'influencers' in my life from fifty years ago. He was an excellent communicator, a Real Estate agent who shared on the art of oral story telling. He was renowned for his creative narratives within our local church community. As he urged our small-interest-group to make sure that we bring the five senses into play; he encouraged us to describe the smells, the sounds, the colours and the tactile sensations, as well as to entice the emotions. *'Draw your listeners / readers in. Not only make them feel the atmosphere within the scenario, but also make them feel the emotions of the characters—the suspense … the fear … the excitement … the sadness etc.'*

My attitude and thinking has changed so much since that time. I've gone from intensely disliking story writing as a child and teenager to now, bursting at the seams in an effort to get my ideas down on paper or screen. And I can only attribute the shift over the years to the face-to-face mentors and the many more silent coaches.

I would also like to acknowledge the pastors of Berwick Church of Christ in the south-east of Melbourne—their creativity in preaching and storytelling is exceptional—with a special shout out to Pastor Michael Rojales. During one of his sermons in 2023, one passing comment was all it took for a new idea to sprout. While speaking about Jesus' miracle of feeding the five thousand, Michael casually remarked, "Can you imagine this little boy saying to his mother and friends: '*He took my lunch!*'" That simple phrase was all that it took to plant the seed of the concept of this book.

I am indebted to Helen Oglivie for her precise scrutiny of the text. Likewise, I am constantly challenged and encouraged by Rod Semple for his 'out-of- left-field' thinking. And lastly, my dear wife Maree, to whom I am so thankful for her unwavering support and encouragement.

Finally, over many years, there have been numerous authors, pastors and motivational speakers who have greatly impacted my creativity, storytelling, thinking and writing… but none more so than El Shaddai—*the All-Sufficient One*—*the God Who is More than Enough!* His creative giftings are immeasurable!

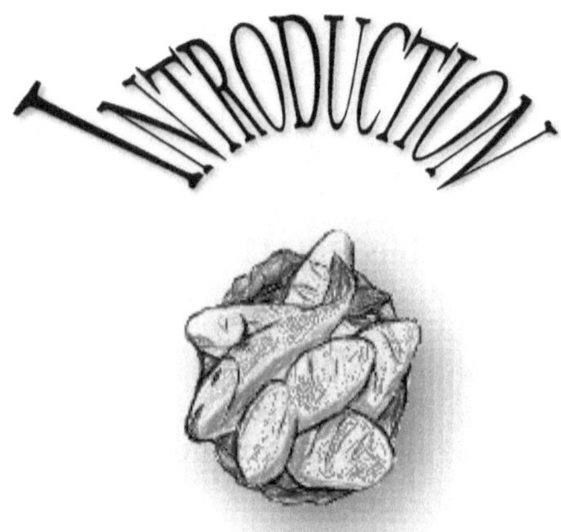

An incident which took place in an isolated place amongst thousands of people changed the life of young Yosef—a nine-year-old boy—forever.

As he listened to the greatest Teacher of all time speak in parables and watched Him perform incredible miracles, Yosef began to realize that, despite his young age, he actually had faith in his heart… faith the size of a mustard seed.

He'd been out all day with his best friend and, like everyone around him, he too was getting hungry, as was Jesus, the Teacher and his disciples. Yosef's small faith was stirred to the point of offering up everything that was in his lunch pack to the Teacher.

He had every confidence that the teacher would know what to do with it.

No doubt you will have heard the old adage: '*do not judge a book by its cover!*' Well, I can guarantee this is certainly true when it comes to choosing this book. The title and the cover are deceptive. It may look like a children's book… and to some extent it may even read like a children's book… but it is definitely not intended to be a children's book!

Even though the story telling style and techniques may appear simplistic and even juvenile at times; I assure you otherwise. Let me explain: '*welcome to my world—this is my style of thinking and writing!*'

The story of '*the feeding of the five thousand*' is a familiar bible story and a children's favourite. Therefore, the reason this book is definitely not written *for* children, is because it contains some specific adult themes and issues.

However, I would still encourage parents and grandparents, as well as Kids' Ministry workers and Christian School teachers, to consider sharing with your children / students very seriously, especially the sections concerning '*the feeding of the five thousand*'. This miracle itself is conveyed from the perspective of young Yosef, who went home and told his mother about how "*He (Jesus) took my lunch!*" I'm sure that it would give any child some fresh insight into this much-loved miracle-story. (* chapters - see contents page)

As you read this book, you will also become fully immersed in a series of speculative backstories woven throughout. According to the synoptic gospels, there was a series of other miraculous events which would have occurred around the same time. Some of these stories, however, would have taken many years of preparation in order for the miraculous outcomes to occur.

My brain is naturally wired to fill the gaps in stories—as in time frames, distances travelled, *'extras'* in the story behind the scenes, meeting places, smells, sounds as well as… emotions.

So, now, here is my disclaimer…

If you consider yourself to be a biblical conservative traditionalist—i.e. a stickler to the text—then as a factual reader you will be challenged in your biblical understanding. I can already hear you saying things like: *"if it's not in the text, then we don't need to know!"* So prepare yourself. You will be compelled to think outside of your strict mindset of *'stick to the text'*. And, more than likely, at some stage you may be tempted to label me a heretic!

You will also be provoked to consider the possibility that each of these miracle stories and the characters involved, may in some way… somehow… be mysteriously interconnected.

For example: have you never wondered about the twelve years of bleeding that caused the woman to reach out to touch the hem of Jesus' garment … and how a twelve-year-old girl (Jairus' daughter) lay dying … all on the same day? The fact is … they did!

Why? How?

Coincidence?! Happenstance?!

Or … were they connected providentially?

I encourage you to read this book with an open mind as you are confronted with such possibilities. I pray too that you may have an open heart to receive some fresh spiritual insights concerning matters of faith, trust, hope and obedience in seeing God's miraculous provision.

Finally, as you read "He Took My Lunch", you will be reminded over and over again, that the One we call Adonai—'the Lord Almighty', is also El Shaddai—'the All-Sufficient One', 'the God Who is more than enough'.

CHAPTER ONE

CAN I GO?

In a small village just south west of the ancient city of Capernaum lived a widow, Miriam, with her ten-year-old son Yosef and her aging mother, Abigail. Their village was one of several villages scattered between Gennesaret and Capernaum. It was the second last village comprising about a dozen small houses not far from Capernaum.

A large, wide-trunked solitary sycamore tree stood with thick, jutting roots almost screening the winding narrow road that ran through the village from south to north, lined by almond and acacia trees scattered among the houses.

Since her husband Jared's sudden passing, Miriam's small household had struggled to survive on the meagre savings he left behind, which she supplemented by baking loaves of bread and selling them in the surrounding villages. Her pantry was also regularly stocked with dried fish, thanks to the generosity of Jared's former fishing buddies.

One early spring morning, the air was crisp, and the sun shone brightly, illuminating the delicate whitish-pink blossoms of the almond trees mixed with the emerging yellow flowers of the acacias. Young Yosef could be seen squatting beneath the sycamore tree just outside his house. He was playing with his clay marbles in the dirt waiting for his friend Asher to arrive. However, this day would turn out to be not just any typical spring day.

Yosef had a slightly pudgy appearance, as if he still retained some baby fat. His tight black hair was always neatly brushed, framing his olive-skinned face. His inquisitive ebony eyes and engaging smile were charmingly emphasized by two missing teeth.

In the distance he could hear his name being called. "Yosef! Yosef! He's coming!" Asher was yelling out as he came running towards the village. Asher lived in the village further north.

"Who's coming Asher?" Yosef quizzed excitedly as he stood to his feet. "Who! Who is coming, chaver?"

Asher and Yosef had been chavers (best friends) since they first met even though Asher was two years older. Asher was taller. A scrawny boy with a mop of uncontrollable brown hair. He always looked out for his younger friend Yosef, whom he called '*Yoyo*'. And Yosef looked up to Asher, who just happened to be the fleetest boy around—swift as a mountain goat and always on the move.

"Jesus, the Teacher, is coming… and his disciples!" shouted Asher. "Come on, Yoyo… let's see if we can find out where they're going!"

"Maybe they'll stop off here in our small village?" Yosef thought to himself as he rushed towards the door of his small village house. Breathlessly, he appealed for his mother's permission to join his friend. "Eema! Eema! Can I go? Everyone else is going?"

"Wait! Where? Go where, Yosef? Slow down, boy" retorted his mother. "Yosef bar Jared… have you forgotten your manners? And where, young man, may I ask is '*everyone else going?*'"

"The Teacher," spluttered Yosef catching his breath. "Jesus and his friends are going to be passing through our village! Asher is running ahead, spreading the good news! Can I go—can *we* go Eema—please?" he begged so impulsively.

"No! My son, *we cannot go*, as your Savta (Grandmother) is not well and I need to stay and care for her," she explained.

Unperturbed, Yosef waited a moment to take in what his mother had just said. Then, in a much more considered way—calmly and respectfully—he asked, "Then *can I* go please, Eema? I promise I will stay close to Asher all the time. *P-l-e-a-s-e*?"

His Eema turned and looked towards her own mother. They locked eyes. She knew exactly what her own Eema was thinking in that moment, with that twinkle in her eye.

She turned back to answer her son, "Well, you'd better make sure that you do, I don't want you getting lost amongst all those people. Do you understand young man?" cautioned his mother. "But before you go, here… take something to eat and make sure you share some with Asher. And keep your eyes open for your Dohd (Uncle) Jairus and your Dodan (cousin) Taliah. Make sure your Dohd knows that you are in the crowd."

"Yes, Eema." She handed him a knapsack full of snacks from the pantry. Yosef grabbed the knapsack and raced towards the door, as she urged him, "And don't be late home!"

"No Eema! Thank you Eema! Love you! Shalom Eema! Shalom Savta!" he called back as he rushed outside.

Stepping out of the doorway into the narrow street, Yosef was almost bowled over by an elderly woman carrying a water pot on her head. "Oh sorry, little boy! Be careful! Watch where you're going!"

The noise of footsteps and excitement grew closer and louder as Yosef squinted his eyes beyond the village gate. "He *is* coming!" Yosef screamed excitedly, jumping up and down. Then, suddenly like a giant wave breaking on the beach, people came rushing toward him with such ferocity that he was forced to jump quickly backward and sideways into the roots of the sycamore tree. He needed to avoid being swept off his feet or, worse still, crushed to death. The people were moving so fast!

Then he had an idea. Initially, for safety reasons he decided to climb up into the sycamore tree as he had many times before, but by doing so it also enabled him to see more clearly into the faces of the moving crowd. But where was Jesus? And, more pressingly right now, where was Asher? Had his friend forgotten all about him? Or had he simply left without him because he'd taken so long pleading for his Eema's permission?

Then suddenly, in amongst the crowd, Yosef spotted Jesus approaching, surrounded by his disciples. Somehow, amidst the swell of all the noise, he heard the Teacher's voice, ever so clearly. He heard Jesus speaking to his closest walking companion. Then, just at that moment as Jesus was approaching where Yosef was hanging out on the limb of the tree, Jesus looked up and winked at him. As he passed underneath the tree, Yosef could hear him saying something about getting to a boat and going to a solitary place. Then, just as clearly, he heard a couple of the outer disciples talking about how upset Jesus had been after finding out about the recent beheading of his cousin, John the Baptiser. And how they hadn't even had a chance to tell the Teacher about all the healings and preaching adventures they had experienced since returning from their two-by-two mission trip. There was so much to share!

Even though they were moving at a steady pace, it was as if Jesus and his close group of companions just passed by in slow motion—slow enough for him to see and hear. Then, as quickly as the mob of people had approached… they were gone. As the dust cloud slowly disappeared into the distance, so too did the noisy cheers, shouting, pushing and scuffling footsteps all drift away.

Just as Yosef climbed down one side of the tree, Asher appeared from the other side, as if out of nowhere. 'Well, are you coming, Yoyo?'

Startled, Yosef's heart skipped a couple of beats. "Oh, *don't do that* Asher. You nearly scared me out of my skin!"

"Well… are you coming or not chaver?" insisted his friend.

Yosef nodded and smiled, but he raised his hand, signalling for his friend to stop and listen for a moment. He wanted to explain what he had just heard as Jesus and the disciples passed by. In response, Asher grabbed Yosef's arm and spun him around in the opposite direction, causing the younger boy to be dizzy with confusion.

"That's great chaver! Come on… let's go Yoyo! Let's take advantage of this… I know a short cut!" declared Asher enthusiastically.

And, just to make sure that the younger boy kept pace with his speedy friend, Yosef held firmly on to his knapsack in one hand, and on to Asher's hand with the other, as they raced off together.

ॐ

CHAPTER TWO

THERE THEY ARE!

They raced back through the small village, veering onto a path that seemed more like a goat track. It was extremely narrow weaving its way through the scrub, which meant that Yosef could no longer hold his friend's hand. Asher was so swift of foot that it seemed his feet were hardly touching the ground. Yosef struggled to keep up with him, as the twisting turns and low-hanging branches made it even harder to avoid tripping or being knocked off his feet.

As they scampered through the scrubby undergrowth, creatures of all kinds scurried off to get out of their way. A young fox taken by surprise leapt vertically off the ground before scrambling away in another direction. A slow-moving turtle on the path forced the boys to leap over the shelled creature. They saw rabbits, hedgehogs, spiny-tailed lizards, quail, badgers and snakes; besides a vast variety of birds taking flight.

After a while, Yosef needed to slow down as he was not as physically agile as Asher. He was out of breath and Asher was out of sight. The only sounds to be heard apart from his own heaving for breath, were the flittering and twittering of birds in the trees.

After a few minutes Asher returned with his leather water bottle. "Here Yoyo—have a drink while you catch your breath. We're nearly there little chaver!" Yosef wondered to himself where 'there' was.

Having caught his breath and gulping some water, they were ready to set out again. Wiping the water drops running down his chin, he took off after Asher with an extra bounce of energy. It seemed like they were heading in a totally different direction. Yosef had no idea where he was, or where they were going. He felt as if he'd been spun about as in a game of blind-man's bluff. But all along, he trusted his older friend implicitly as they headed further into the unknown scrub.

"Hey Asher, can we slow down a bit, please? yelled Yosef. "Besides, I thought you said we were nearly there!" For Yosef, what seemed like hours had in fact only been about forty-five minutes.

"We *are!* We are *here!* Come on Yoyo, look there!" exclaimed Asher, whilst slowing to a walking pace. They exited the scrub of undulating forest just in time to catch up with the tail end of the party of determined followers in pursuit of the Teacher. However, it wasn't long before the boys realised that everyone had come to an abrupt halt and a hush had swept over the group. They stood watching Jesus and his disciples climb into a couple of boats on the beach down below.

"Let's go Yoyo, before we miss them altogether!" asserted Asher, despite having no idea of where they would be heading. But the younger boy grabbed hold of his friend and whispered, "Remember, I told you that I'd heard Jesus say as they passed by my house something about going to a quiet solitary place! There's a place like that just outside Bethsaida. I know… because my Abba took me there before he died last year!"

[Yosef's father had been a fisherman who, unfortunately, accidentally slipped overboard and became entangled in the fishing net. He struggled to free himself, but the more he fought, the more ensnared he became. By the time his fishing buddies reached him and managed to unravel the net, it was too late—he had drowned.]

"Yes!" mouthed Asher silently as he punched his fist in the air. "Ok, let's go!" Then to everyone's astonishment, at the top of his voice he screamed out announcing, "This way everybody… they're heading for Bethsaida!"

The leading group of followers then had to scramble back up the steep cliff from the beach, and so they became the tail-end of the party, as Asher and Yosef were now in the leading group.

They had not gone very far when they came to the Chorazin-Bethsaida fork in the road. Then, to everyone's surprise they were joined by hundreds more people. The crowd had grown like a snowball rolling down a slope. From Yosef's village of a couple of hundred pilgrims the group had grown to now, what seemed like thousands!

As they plodded along, Yosef was intrigued to see how many sick people were being carried on stretchers, cripples were hobbling along with crutches, blind people being led along by the arm, children with palsy being wheeled along in wooden wheelbarrows, as well as old and frail people being supported by their family or friends. There were others who were very bent over although they could walk, and some who were obviously disturbed or tormented in their minds, randomly screaming out expletives and curses.

The multitude seemed to be swelling in number. There were families, farmers, pharisees, peasants and high-profile dignitaries—all with one common purpose. They were seeking not only to be present when the Teacher began his teaching… but also to receive, or to see a miraculous healing from the hands and words of the Great Physician—Jesus of Nazareth.

As they travelled along, Yosef was so glad that they did not have to run, but they certainly had to walk fast to keep pace with the able-bodied adults in the increasing crowd of followers. As they steadily kept pace, Yosef reached into his knapsack and pulled out two small loaves of bread and a couple of small, dried fish. He gave one to Asher and, in turn, his friend handed him the leather water bottle to wash down their snack.

Following the coast they managed to keep sight of the boats for quite some time. However, as the coastline rose higher, it became harder to make out the vessels against the glistening of the sun on the water. Then, as if time stood still for some reason, the light suddenly changed, and the town of Bethsaida came into view. The company of walkers knew that they needed to bypass the township in order to get to the grassy knoll between the beach and the town.

As the troupe rounded the bend heading away from the township, they were joined by several hundred more people, all with the same intent. Once again, those at the forefront could see the boats. They could see that Jesus and his disciples had beached their boats and were heading up the embankment towards the grassy knoll.

Jesus and his friends had only just settled down when, from out of nowhere and from every direction a multitude of people swarmed towards them. The disciples appeared to be annoyed and a bit overwhelmed by the sheer number of people. It was about the sixth hour —midday.

CHAPTER THREE

A MIRACLE on the DOORSTEP

All along the way, Yosef had been constantly scanning the crowd trying to find his Dohd (Uncle) Jairus and his (Dodan) Cousin Tahlia, but without success.

A few weeks earlier, Yosef's cousin, Tahlia, had been the subject of one of Jesus' healing miracles in Capernaum. He was absolutely certain that they would be amongst this large gathering somewhere.

His Dodah (Aunt) Eunice—just like his own Eema—unfortunately would be at home, caring for her aging mother-in-law.

His Dohd Jairus—being a synagogue ruler in Capernaum—would be easily recognised by his distinguishable garments and head covering; and his cousin, having the deepest auburn hair—long and very curly, would also certainly stand out.

Jairus and Eunice had been unable to have children. They had prayed for many years but, for whatever reason only known to God, He had not yet answered their prayers. They were fast approaching middle age.

Then late one night, after many years of faithfully praying for a child, Eunice woke up suddenly from a dream. She felt that the Lord had woken her up to go and look on the doorstep of the synagogue. She quickly woke her husband and told him about her dream. Together they walked next door, and there on the doorstep of the synagogue was a small bundle wrapped in a blanket. Eunice picked it up and immediately felt the movement of a baby's body shivering from the cold. As she carefully unfolded the outer layer of the exotic-cloth-blanket, a little baby gave a whimper which quickly turned into a squawking cry of hunger. The couple looked at each other with intense wonder and joy before quickly turning their heads to see if anyone was lurking in the shadows. Aside from Eunice's soothing shushes, the baby's cries, and their own heavy breathing, there was no other movement or sound to be heard.

Not wanting to wake their neighbours, they quickly retreated into their house and closed the door. Once inside, they were able to see under the light of the lantern, that they were holding a perfect baby girl with distinctive tight curly reddish hair. A scrawly note fell from the unfolded blanket. It read: *'Trust in the Lord with all your heart. Do not lean on your own understanding. In all your ways acknowledge him, and he will direct your paths.'*

They both immediately knelt and praised God for His miraculous provision for their childless-aching hearts after so long. As they worshipped the Lord together, the baby quietened down and slept peacefully in Eunice's arms.

What happened next was indeed another miracle. Within minutes of getting up from the floor, Eunice felt a flooding sensation within her breasts.

Immediately, Eunice sat down on a chair, unfolded her gown and placed one of her nipples gently near the baby's lips. Without any hesitation the baby began suckling. Milk flowed through her breasts from that moment and continued every day until it was time to wean the child.

Within a few days news had spread of this wonderful provision from the Lord. Of course, there was much speculation as to where the child had come from. Who was the mother? Who was the father? Who had placed the child on the doorstep? What had happened to the mother? And, naturally, what would they name this little girl?

There was much hearsay about possible answers to these unanswerable questions, and there were equally many suggestions of girls' names. Jairus and Eunice were not in a hurry to name their new daughter, but they both knew in their hearts what God was saying. So when it was time, they presented her before the Lord in the synagogue and named her Taliah meaning: *'dew of God; flourishing, blooming'.*

Tahlia grew to become a beautiful child, full of joy and laughter, and good company to her adoptive parents. Her hair deepened in colour along with her curls, which puzzled many people as to her true parentage.

As she grew physically, so did her parents' concern for her health, possibly as a result of having been abandoned on their doorstep in the cold. Taliah was a frail child. She very easily became short of breath and often found breathing quite difficult. And to complicate things even more, she frequently ran out of energy, which meant that she was restricted in how far from home she could go and the activities she could undertake. Yet, she remained joyful and grateful for her parents' loving care.

Taliah would often ask her Eema and Abba to tell her the story of how they'd found her on the doorstep. She loved to hear of their faithful prayers to Adonai and how he had blessed them by keeping her safe and alive. She especially loved the part of how God had miraculously provided milk for her through her adoptive mother. She never grew tired of listening to her parents tell the story but, as she grew in years, she too began to form many questions about her heritage. Questions like: *Where was she born? What was her mother like? Why was she abandoned? Who was her father? Were her birth parents still alive, and if so where were they?*

Taliah's quest for knowledge of the Jewish faith impressed her Eema and Abba. Even more so since neither of them knew the answers to their daughter's deep questions about her origins. Yet, as she approached puberty, those questions began to burn even more deeply within her. They became like a burdensome weight within her heart and mind. After her first menstrual cycle, it started to take its toll on her both physically and emotionally. It was slowly draining the life out of her. However, it was more than that… much more like a spiritual burden weighing heavily upon her.

Jairus and his small family had heard many stories about Jesus of Nazareth. They were in the synagogue when Jesus was first invited to read from the scriptures, and they'd witnessed him heal a man who had a withered arm—a man they actually had known for years! Jairus was also present on the day when Jesus was teaching at Simon's house, when some men cleared an opening in the roof. They could not get their crippled friend into the house due to the number of people. So they'd decided to lower him down through the ceiling in order for Jesus to heal him. Dust and straw rained down from the ceiling onto those inside. Jairus was aware that the Pharisees and Sadducees were adamantly opposed to Jesus' teachings and especially his healing of people during Shabbat. Yet secretly, Jairus was impressed with what he had heard the Teacher say and seen him do.

Eunice and Jairus could only watch and pray as they sat by their daughter's bedside watching as life drained out of her body. Word had spread that Jesus and his disciples were returning to Capernaum following one of their missions. As his daughter became weaker by the hour, Jairus was beside himself with fear that his daughter would die. He knew that he had to do something quickly and the only thing he could think of was to reach out in faith to the

Teacher, to come and heal his daughter. "Eunice, I'm going to find Jesus!" he called out as he left.

Hurrying out of the house he headed towards Simon's house, only to find out that Jesus and his disciples were not yet back. Someone suggested they were still on the seashore. He sped off as fast as he could with his robes flowing in the wind.

On approaching the beach, Jairus could see that Jesus was surrounded by hundreds of people. Undeterred, he hastily moved down and pushed his way unapologetically into and through the crowd towards him.

Out of breath, without any sense of dignity or hesitation, Jairus fell at Jesus' feet, begging Him to come and heal his daughter. "Teacher, my daughter is dying! She's only twelve years old! If you would please come to my house and just place your hands on her, I believe that she will live!"

Helping Jairus to his feet, Jesus put his arm around him as he whispered something in his ear. Together they began walking up the beach towards Jairus' home. As they did so, the anticipation and excitement throughout the crowd of onlookers was palpable. The disciples struggled to keep the throng from pressing in too close or, worse still causing some kind of public stampede where people might be crushed to death. Slowly but surely as they walked towards Jairus' house, there was some sort of disturbance coming from behind. Jesus stopped to look around.

Jairus felt both frustrated and concerned. Would this unexpected interruption create a delay that might mean Jesus would not reach his daughter in time? Would she die?

Jairus was close by Jesus and stood there in amazement as the Healer showed compassion to someone else in the pressing crowd who had touched his garment.

The disciples, on the other hand, were very much aware of the watchfulness of Roman soldiers and the ramifications of causing a disturbance. They breathed a sigh of relief, however, as they witnessed Jesus take complete control of what was unfolding before their very eyes, right in the middle of the crowded street… and not a single soldier in view!

LOVE at FIRST SIGHT

Being under Roman rule meant that Jewish people were constantly under the strict scrutiny of soldiers. Every soldier in Capernaum was under orders to take control of any public disturbances which may lead to populace unrest. Roman soldiers were stationed throughout the whole of Israel and beyond. The forces consisted of foot legionnaires to mounted soldiers and archers, and were specifically accountable to their supervising centurion overseeing approximately one hundred soldiers.

Legionary soldiers were recruited from the age of seventeen years. Part of their ruthless training was to stand their ground, without showing fear or any other emotion. They were certainly discouraged from fraternising with the sub-class of Jews, in fact they would be severely reprimanded if they were found to be friendly with any Jew.

Approximately thirteen years before Jairus' plea for Jesus to come and heal his daughter at Capernaum, there was a young Roman soldier named Dimitrius who had just turned eighteen years of age. He was living in Jerusalem at the time, although his ancestral roots went back to the Gauls. He was very handsome, well built and tall. His reddish hair, which he kept very short, was mostly covered by his helmet. Since he'd been recruited for military service, he was in training for officer rank of Tesserarius—as second in command to an Optio officer.

His first posting was in Jerusalem, under the watchful eye of his father, who was stationed there as Legate—a high-ranking Roman military officer overseeing numerous centurions. Part of this scrutiny was complicated by the fact that they made every effort to keep their relationship concealed.

One afternoon in late Spring, Dimitrius and several of his comrades were patrolling one of the market places in the Jewish capital, not far from the temple. It was a maze of stalls peddling all sorts of wares from fruit and vegetables, fish and meat, herbs and spices, pots and pans to cloths and dyes.

Wandering through the market stalls allowed any of these soldiers carte blanche to anything they fancied—whether it be a piece of fruit or a kitchen utensil. The Jewish stall holders generally would never challenge this theft of their produce for fear of some verbal or physical reprisal.

On this particular sunny afternoon, Dimitrius and one of his fellow soldiers approached a bread stall selling a variety of loaves. His companion decided that he would help himself to a seeded loaf of bread. Snatching the loaf he ripped it apart, took a large bite and then threw the broken pieces onto the ground. Sparrows and chooks scurried over to feast on the discarded bread, causing such a cacophony of squawking and squabbling over every large and tiny morsel.

The stall holder happened to be a young feisty teenage girl about seventeen years of age selling the bread that her grandparents had baked. She took umbrage at this theft, as it was the first time she had seen her grandfather's hard work being taken advantage of so blatantly. Her name was Mara, and she also happened to be stunningly beautiful with deep brown eyes, a flawless olive complexion and thick curly black hair noticeably sticking out from under her headscarf.

"Hey soldier!" she challenged assertively. "Show some respect for quality baking will you!? This good bread has been baked by my Saba for human consumption, not for dogs or birds!" Immediately, others nearby gasped in trepidation as they stopped what they were doing to see what would happen next.

Dimitrius approached the offending soldier, and immediately his gaze was drawn to Mara. In that moment, their eyes engaged intensely as he leaned over to whisper into his comrade's ear, *"Noli respicere post tergum."*

Gently, but firmly, he took hold of the offending soldier's arm and led him away before his associate could retaliate in any way. For the briefest of moments, as Dimitrius engaged with Mara's eyes, it was as if time stood still and their souls became enmeshed beyond words.

For both of them, it seemed they were able to see deeply into the other's soul, far beyond that which they could actually appreciate of their own individual natural beauty or handsomeness. They felt so connected in that instant of time and realised they had to meet privately—but how?… when?… where?

The two soldiers left without any further incident, leaving Mara standing there like a marble sculpture. Everyone around her, including stall holders and customers, quietly cheered before returning to what they had been doing previously.

ひ

CHAPTER FIVE

SECRET RENDEZVOU

Mara slowly regained her focus on working at the bread stall, yet all the while, she found herself wondering about what had happened just moments before. About thirty minutes later, a young boy came to the stall and handed her a note. It was from Dimitrius—though he had not signed his name for security reasons. She opened the note and read the scrawled letters: '*Please, meet me tonight at the twelfth hour (after sunset) in the garden between Hezekiah's tunnel and Gihon Spring*'.

She held the note close to her heart realising that, although neither of them knew the other's name, they had been instantaneously bound in love and, by some strange force… they were meant to be together. But what would her Saba and Savta say if they found out?

Mara had been raised by her grandparents from the age of five, since her parents had been tragically killed when the tower of Siloam fell. She owed her life to her Saba and Savta but, even so, she vowed to herself not to say anything to her grandparents about what had happened earlier. She certainly hoped that no-one else would either. She knew she needed to keep this a secret—at least for the time being.

Their rendezvous went ahead without any detection, although seeing Dimitrius incognito—dressed in civilian clothes—took a few moments for her mind to adjust in the moonlight. As they embraced each other for the first time, hardly a word was spoken between them. So great was their passion, they gave themselves to each other without restraint or shame.

Time seemed simply to fade into oblivion yet, as they gathered their thoughts and awareness of their surroundings and their garments, they agreed to meet again the following night. Night after night, for about the next month, they continued to come together. Sometimes they simply canoodled and shared stories as they lay on the ground staring at the stars, and other times they gave in to their passionate love for each other. At long last it became evident that they needed to communicate with more than just dreamy romantic words and their infatuation for passionate sensual alliance.

After their greeting of embrace one warm evening, Mara stood apart from her lover. Dimitrius sensed something was in the air and waited. She hesitantly informed him that she was pregnant.

There was a pronounced silence in response for a few brief moments, which seemed like an eternity to Mara. Then Dimitrius began speaking in unemotional monotones. He was resolute and calculated in his response. And although he would not show any type of feeling—not joy, excitement or surprise—to this news, deep within his heart and mind he was shocked and afraid of what this would mean for his chances of promotion through the ranks. This would indeed be scandalous… a Roman officer fathering a Jewish girl's child.

To add confusion to Mara's dilemma, without any emotional attachment whatsoever, Dimitrius warned her not to say anything to anyone and that he needed some time to figure out what to do. There was no further discussion and certainly no sexual encounter that evening, just an embrace and a kiss goodnight.

It was decided that they would not meet up again until Dimitrius had figured out a plan. Mara went home wondering what he had in mind but, because she loved him, she decided not to become anxious about what might happen next… but that wasn't to be. Struggling to sleep, her escalating thoughts reeled about on what might happen to their relationship?… what would happen to her?… how long would it be before her Savta began to notice?… what would be her grandparents' reaction?… what would happen to Dimitrius? Then the real cruncher… what would happen to her baby? So many questions and so little sleep.

THE VOICE OF COMMAND

The following morning, after a sleepless night, Dimitrius went to speak to his father in private but, of course, he needed to be in uniform. In order to get past the security guards he'd concocted a story on the pretence that he needed to report some secret threat of uprising within his sector of the city.

The security guards ushered him into the Legate's meeting chamber and stood waiting for instructions. As this was the first time that Dimitrius had formally requested an audience with his father in this way, the high-ranking officer sensed the need for privacy and so he dismissed the guards and ordered them to close the doors behind them. Sensing an urgency of importance, the father indicated to his son to have a seat.

In a calm and quiet tone of voice his father questioned: "What is it my son? I know that you are not here to report such an uprising! What is on your mind… tell me!"

Dimitrius took a deep breath and swallowed hard as he plucked up the courage to speak. As this was not a military interview, but rather a father-son dialogue, he opened his mouth and began stumbling over his words. Showing restraint, his father lovingly said, "Come on Dim… spit it out!"

From that point, the young man explained everything from the day in the market place, the secret note and subsequent rendezvous up until last evening's disclosure. He expressed his deep love for Mara. He confessed the painful realization that by his actions, he had tarnished his family's name and could potentially jeopardise his father's reputation. He was utterly bewildered about what to do next.

Dimitrius' father shuffled in his seat. The son waited. In the sterility of this room not a thing was out of place. His father looked at the tiled floor for some time then, standing to his feet, he stepped back into his commanding role of Legate. *"On your feet, soldier!"* At once, Dimitrius stood to attention.

In a very controlled voice of command he spoke. "We need to put this issue to rest quickly and quietly. You have indeed brought great shame to our family's name, but *you are* my son!" The Legate paused and took in breath. Holding back any hint of emotion he slightly increased the volume and pitch of his voice. "As far as your officership goes—you have disgraced yourself… your rank… your troop… and Cesear! You will be redeployed to another province on probation for three months."

Then, lowering his voice of command once again, "As for this girl, are you certain that you are the father?" Dimitrius nodded "Yes, sir, one hundred percent. She is not that sort of girl! And besides… I love her!"

"Son, you will need to dismiss this idea of love!" Without showing any further sign of emotion his father instructed him. "Here is what you are to do… and without question. You will arrange a secret meeting and tell her that she needs to see someone to abort the child. If she refuses to do so, then you must send her away to Galilee, or even further. Either way, you will provide for her the money she needs…

for whichever cause of action she decides." Then straightening his stance and increasing the volume of his voice, the commanding father questioned, "Is this understood Legionary?"

"Yes Legate!" Dimitrius reported.

His father leaned over to take something out of his desk. He handed his son three hundred denarii explaining that the amount was pertinent to the period of their liaison—ten denarii or ten days' wages—for each night they had spent together. Upon doing so, the father embraced his son and whispered, "You *will* be missed."

Quickly stepping back into military mode and, with one final announcement, the Legate declared: "Legionary Dimitrius, as of tomorrow you will be posted to Galatia. Your deployment papers will be prepared immediately. *Noli respicere post tergum.* Dismissed!"

Dimitrius turned and marched out of his father's office, and his life, for a very long time. He immediately went to the barracks to pack his belongings, but before leaving he sat and scribbled one last note to Mara.

℘

CHAPTER SEVEN

THAT'S NOT A CHOICE!

They met at the same place at the same time as they had done so since they had begun seeing each other. However, this was to be a very different encounter than their first, apart from the tentative kiss and embrace. Mara's heart pounded in anticipation as to what her lover would have planned out for them. And Dimitrius appeared stoically calm and controlled on the outside, whilst being nervously petrified on the inside.

Mara cautiously asked him, "What's your plan for us Dim… and our baby? What are we going to…?" but before she could continue, he tenderly put his finger on her lips. She stopped.

Taking a deep breath, he spoke of his report to his father—explaining the fragility of the situation because of his father's rank and high-profile position. "So what did he say Dim? Tell me!" she demanded as her voice became shrill.

Dimitrius gave account of his father's reaction to the situation and outlined what was required to take care of everything. Firstly, he spoke of his deployment to another province, but he did not say where because he would not officially find out until the next morning.

"But, Dim, what about us? We love each other! We are meant to be together! I can't just simply uproot from here and leave my family and friends to be with you and raise our baby!"

"About the baby," interjected Dimitrius.

"*Our* baby!" Mara corrected him.

"You have a choice," he continued to explain more sternly.

"I have a *choice*, you say?!" she retorted.

"You can choose to find someone who will assist in terminating the pregnancy, or… "

Mara interjected assertively. "No! Dimitrius! That is not a choice, it's a sin against my God!"

"Or… you will need to leave here as soon as possible and go to Galilee. Whatever your decision is, I have provided sufficient money for you until this passes over," he concluded.

"Passes over?!' Mara stepped away and began pacing about in circles, red-faced, arms thrashing, feet stomping and tears gushing. "No Dim! I love you… and no matter what… I would never abort or abandon my baby… *our* baby!"

Dimitrius took a step closer to her and embraced her shaking, trembling body as she wept bitterly, although she tried to push him away. He gently held her close until her sobbing and shaking subsided. He kissed her on the forehead as he placed into her hands a bag of coins, and whispered, "I'm so sorry Mara. *Noli respicere post tergum.*"

He made an about-face, as in military style, and began marching away... leaving her standing there all alone.

Mara struggled to grasp the possibility that this could be the last time they would ever be together intimately—or even see each other.

She turned away… shocked, and in tears, unable to comprehend what had just taken place. She felt abandoned, demeaned and betrayed. And what did Dimitrius mean when he said *"Noli respicere post tergum.?"* She was unfamiliar with this term… even though she recalled hearing it the first day they'd met.

CHAPTER EIGHT

THIS IS OUR CHOICE

Mara ran all the way home to her grandparents. The house was filled with the smells of rising dough and baking bread. She burst into the small kitchen where her Saba and Savta were preparing for the next day and collapsed into her Savta's arms. She sobbed uncontrollably, quickly saturating her Savta's apron with tears.

As her sobbing waned, her Saba came and sat down at the table and held her hand. Lifting her head he lovingly asked her about what had happened to cause such a display of tears. "Is there a boy that has broken your heart, my sweet girl?" her grandfather compassionately asked.

With the subsiding of her tears, she looked them both in the eye and retold the whole story from beginning to end. "I'm really sorry Saba, Savta. I have dishonoured you and I have sinned against Adonai! I don't know what to do. I'm so sorry. I should have told you earlier. My heart became utterly enthralled with infatuation the moment Dimitrius first looked into my eyes.

Her Savta continued to hold her hands in comforting reassurance, whilst Saba withdrew from her in silence. Mara squeezed her grandmother's hand for reassurance but it seemed that Saba was about to speak, so she remained silent.

Saba stood to his feet and paced the floor, then he fell to his knees as he ripped open his outer garment and cried aloud a range of indecipherable sounds. He reached over to the fire place and picked up some of the ashes and sprinkled them over his head. He wept and wailed, then laid down prostrate on the kitchen floor in prayerful anguish. As a deeply devout Jew his heart was torn apart. And being head of the family, he pleaded to Adonai for wisdom to know what to say and what to do in this situation.

Mara and Savta also wept silently as this remorsefully tragic scene unfolded before their eyes. Saba's wailing became less vociferous, yet he continued to lay there motionless for several more minutes. Eventually he gathered himself and struggling to his feet, made his way back to the table.

He sat silently as he gazed into the loving face of his wife of more than forty years, then he shifted his eyes towards his granddaughter. His eyes appeared glazed over from the tears. Then he turned as he noticed the bag of coins on the table for the first time.

He chose his words carefully and spoke with such tenderness and compassion towards Mara. "My dear girl. This situation is extremely difficult—it is almost impossible for us to comprehend what you have just disclosed.

"Since your parents were taken from us so suddenly, your Savta and I have committed ourselves to raise you as our own child. We vowed to the Lord that we would teach you to respect and obey the Torah and the ways of being Jewish. We have prayed for you, cared for you, laughed with you and cried with you. We have always loved you—and we will always love you." He tentatively placed his hand on his wife's hand which was still holding onto Mara's.

After pausing for a deep breath, he removed his hand and continued speaking. "You were correct when you confessed that you have sinned before Adonai. You have disobeyed the Torah. And you have dishonoured your parents and, even more so, you have brought shame to Savta and me."

"You say that you are in love with this gentile, Dimitrius—I am not questioning that." Then he turned his eyes towards the bag of coins, and then slowly back to Mara. "The way it seems to me, is that by his offering of this money to do *whichever you choose*… in its crudest form… is equivalent to him simply paying for your services. In abandoning you, it was as if he had labelled you a prostitute… by paying you off in order to keep your silence or to simply disappear."

Following a couple of deep breaths, Saba became even more serious in his tone. "Now, as far as the Torah is concerned, the elders and priests, Pharisees and Sadducees would be justified in having you publicly shamed—excommunicated, beaten or even worse still—stoned to death."

Mara's posture stiffened as she tried to remove her hand from Savta's, but her grandmother held tightly refusing to lose her grip.

"My dear Mara—*our* dear girl. This breaks our hearts—even more so than your heart is broken and betrayed by this young soldier. You have betrayed our trust, but you will never lose our love," he continued, as tears slowly trickled down his cheeks. "Our love for you and your child will continue to be unwavering. Yet, we too have a choice to make just like you, don't we my love?" he said as his eyes engaged his wife's.

She nodded in agreement, then spoke for the first time, sensing her husband's permission to take over for a bit. "Mara, your Saba is a righteous man. His desire is to always honour Adonai with his whole heart, mind and strength. There is no way that he, *that we*, would want you to be either publicly shamed or worse, as Saba has already explained to you. But he is right in saying that *we* also have a choice in what we do. Do you understand Mara?"

Mara whispered, "I think so Savta, but can you please tell me what *your* choice is?"

Her grandmother continued. "Saba could either choose to go to the elders and tell them the situation as it happened, and plead your case. Or, he could choose not to say anything."

Mara turned and peered enquiringly into her grandfather's weary face.

"On the other hand," Savta went on. "Your Saba and I *could* choose to disown you, and demand that you leave our home." Then she paused and looked to the side as if she'd heard a noise.

"Are they the only choices there are Saba … Savta?" she begged her grandparents.

Her grandfather took the lead again. "Mara. Our dearest Mara. With Adonai as our witness… *we* also have a choice to support you, care for you and your baby when it arrives, and that is what we choose." Savta agreed and said, "We are a family and always will be."

The three of them embraced each other for a very long time.

☙

CHAPTER NINE

REVEALED IN A DREAM

Mara slept very soundly that night, the first time since she had met Dimitrius, and feeling very grateful for such loving grandparents. However, during the night as she dreamt, she had a vision of herself travelling to Galilee and giving birth to her child as a way of protecting her grandparents from shame. The voice in her dream spoke clearly, telling her that this was *her* choice, and if she decided to proceed, further instructions would come when she needed them.

As she began waking from her dream, she heard the voice quoting one of King Solomon's Proverbs: *'Trust in the Lord with all your heart. Do not lean on your own understanding. In all your ways acknowledge him, and he will direct your paths.'*

She rose from her bed before her Saba and Savta and cooked them a simple breakfast. As they woke and came into the kitchen, they saw a radiant and peaceful young woman.

Sitting down together to break their nightly fast, Mara shared with her grandparents details of her dream. They listened intently as she explained why she had decided to go to Galilee—not because of what Dimitrius had told her—but because of Adonai's instructions in her dream, and her deep love and respect for both of them.

A different range of emotions to those expressed the night before unfolded in response. Neither of her grandparents tried to dissuade her from her choice to distance herself from them as she embarked on this next season of her life.

They expressed with full confidence that Adonai would protect her and her child and that, in His time, He would bring them home safely.

In practical terms, they discussed her financial needs and realised that in Adonai's providence, nothing is wasted. In fact He had already provided more than enough for her financially.

They prayed a blessing over each other, intermingled with faith and hope amidst tears of sadness and joy. Mara packed some necessities and headed off along the trail towards Galilee.

After travelling for some distance, she met up with some fellow travellers headed for Chorazin, so they journeyed together. Her confidence was boosted by the company of travellers, and she felt reassured of Adonai's protection.

Several hours into their journey, their caravan of travellers was overtaken by a company of Roman soldiers on horseback. Mara wondered in her heart if Dimitrius was one of them, but then she gathered her thoughts together and meditated on the message of the Proverb she had been given in her dream.

∝

Upon her arrival in Chorazin, she went to the market place and sought work on a stall which sold cloth from the orient. The stall holder was a widow named Sarah, who also kindly offered Mara accommodation as part of her wages.

As time went on, her body began to show signs of her baby's development. Sarah graciously accepted Mara's condition without question or disdain—whilst others were very quick to express their scornful distaste. However, Mara continued to feel loved, protected and provided for—all the while knowing that her grandparents were praying for her and her baby.

As her childbirth approached, Sarah arranged for a midwife to stay with Mara when the time came for the baby's delivery. Although Mara felt apprehensive about the birthing process, she found peace within herself, reassured by the Lord's guidance and provision.

The night before she went into labour, Mara initially found it difficult to lie comfortably, but eventually, sleep came relatively easily. Then, as she'd been foretold in a dream from several months earlier, she experienced another dream. In this dream, she was told that her Savta was near death and that her Saba was struggling to cope. She was instructed to return to Jerusalem as soon as possible after the birth of her child.

After such a disturbing dream, she awoke in a deep sweat, her heart racing. Again Adonai had gone before her. Mara was anxious to see her grandparents again, but realising she was very close to giving birth, she reminded herself of the proverb—which brought her comfort and strength.

The next day, Mara gave birth to a beautiful baby girl. Her daughter had olive skin, reddish hair like her father and tiny tight curls like hers. She held her baby close to her breast and felt the motherly instinct and joy of feeding her newborn. She thought of her grandparents… and she thought of Dimitrius.

The midwife carefully explained to Mara that, although the birth went well itself, there was a slight complication with her lochia [the vaginal discharge after giving birth]. She then assured her that she should be fine by the end of the required weeks of purification. However, Mara determined in her heart that she would only wait two weeks before venturing back home to her grandparents.

Having said goodbye to Sarah two weeks later, Mara headed off carrying her sweet little girl—as yet unnamed. For the first part of her journey, it was just her and the baby. Then, from out of nowhere, she was aware of someone walking beside her. "Don't be afraid Mara. I have a message for you from Adonai."

Although startled, she immediately sensed peace in knowing the Lord's presence. The stranger spoke in calm tones of reassurance of comfort and guidance. "You *will* see your grandparents again, but they will not get to see their granddaughter."

Mara broke down in tears. "What! How can this be Lord?" she cried. "Why? What is going to happen to my child?"

"Mara, you have been chosen to carry this child for another. A woman who has been childless for many years and has faithfully prayed all that time to be a mother. When you made the choice to be with Dimitrius, it was not Adonai's choice for you. However, despite that, He has chosen to answer the prayer of this woman and her husband through you. They will adopt your baby and will love her as their own. They will protect her, teach her the ways of the Lord, and they will be the ones to name her with a name that Adonai will show to them."

As she stumbled along, blinking through her tears and trying to process this deeply disturbing information, she sensed a reassuring peace wash over her. She questioned her companion. "So, you are saying that Adonia will take the choices I have made and redeem them for His good purposes? But how will I know what to do?… where to go?… who to speak to?"

The visitor stopped…and taking her by the hand, he placed his hand on the baby's forehead. "Yes, Mara, Adonai knows all things… He sees all things. He will go with you… and before you to prepare this couple. All you have to do is be obedient to His will. Tonight as you pass through Capernaum, even though it will be dark, go to the synagogue. There will be a light in the window for you to see. Place your baby on the doorstep wrapped up tightly. Leave her there, in Adonai's care… then walk away! *Noli respicere post tergum*—do not look back… for if you choose to look back …"

Mara immediately thought, "'*Noli respicere post tergum!* Do not look back. So that's what that means!"

"Wait!" She interjected. "Are you saying that I might turn into a pillar of salt like Lots' wife?" There was almost a note of cynicism with a slight hint of humour in her voice. The visitor continued, "For if you choose to look back… there will be lasting consequences about which I am not permitted to speak about. Remember Mara… *His* will… in *His* way… in *His* time."

They started walking again ever so slowly, but then as she turned to say one last thing… the stranger had disappeared. She stopped, looking in every direction, but could only see someone riding on a camel further ahead.

THIRTY DAYS
OF MOURNING

Mara did as the mysterious visitor had instructed her to do. With a deep reluctance and a bitter sadness in her heart, she sobbed as she kissed her baby daughter one last time, praying for Adonai's protection over their life. She placed her wrapped in the exotic cloth and left as quickly as she could, without being seen. However, as she reached the end of the main street, she could not resist the urge to look back.

The moment she turned around, she saw a woman and a man bending down to cradle her crying child. She quickly turned again and headed off to find a safe place to rest her weary body for the night. She found it extremely difficult to settle her saddened heart. She closed her teary eyes and pondered as to what would happen as a consequence of her turning back to look.

Several days later upon arriving home in Jerusalem, she was greeted by her grandparents with open arms. They were perplexed however… even distressed about the whereabouts of her baby. Mara could tell immediately that her Savta was not very well. Although she was weak and frail, unable to move about freely, she was indeed overjoyed to see her granddaughter again.

Filled with joy at seeing her grandparents again, Mara sat on Savta's bed. Saba brought in some broth and bread for her to eat. She told them everything in every detail. The people she met along the way… her job and her landlady. She went on to tell them about every aspect of her more recent dreams. She explained about the visitor from out of nowhere who knew everything about her story. The only detail she did not tell them was about the warning she'd been given to not look back. She thought it best to leave out that detail for now.

Her grandparents had so many questions, the three of them talked late into the night as they laughed and cried together. But as Saba needed to rise up early and head off to the market, they said their goodnights and headed for bed.

With each new day Savta grew weaker and weaker. About a month later, she did not wake up. Mara and her Saba knelt beside the bed and wept bitterly. Together they arranged the *shiva* (funeral) for later that day, and prepared themselves for the *shloshim*–thirty days of mourning.

It was during this season of mourning that Mara became aware that something was not quite right with her body. Her menstrual cycle had begun once more, but somehow the bleeding was different. It was like what she'd had with the lochia bleeding from the afterbirth. She decided not to say anything to her Saba though.

Throughout their official season of grief Saba and Mara were greatly supported by neighbours and friends who brought food and comfort. Both grandfather and granddaughter drew strength from each other and from the Lord.

Once the period of *shloshim* had concluded they went back to work, baking and selling their loaves of bread. They enjoyed working together but, as time went on, Mara became more aware that something was not right within her body. She spoke with her grandfather about finding a doctor or midwife who might be able to help, but this would cost money. Fortunately, though, she had left some of the money she received from Dimitrius with her grandparents for safe keeping.

The doctors and midwives whom she'd located in Jerusalem unfortunately could not help her—although they were happy to take her money. Month after month, year after year she continued searching for someone who could diagnose her ailment and provide treatment.

℘

After about twelve years of enduring the pain and discomfort of this issue, another incident brought even more sadness to Mara. Her Saba suddenly dropped dead in the kitchen whilst he was mixing up bread dough.

Mara felt devastated and alone. As she isolated herself throughout another season of mourning, she pondered what would become of her. She was fast approaching thirty years of age and, because of her bleeding issue, she had resolved herself to the fact that she would never be able to marry or have any more children. In the eyes of the Law and the Jewish people… she knew she would be considered unclean; but it was becoming much more difficult to conceal the odour.

Then one day in the market place she heard people talking about a healer—a teacher—who some said was Yeshua Moshia'—Jesus the Saviour. She'd heard stories of miraculous healings before, but these were different. Deaf people having their ears unblocked. Blind people having their eyes opened. Demoniacs were being delivered and set free from their tormentors. Lepers were healed and reinstated as 'clean.'

It was the word 'clean' that spoke to her, as she suddenly remembered the moment she looked back after depositing her baby girl on the doorstep of the synagogue in Capernaum.

Upon hearing that Jesus of Nazareth was in Capernaum, a surge of clarity washed over her, and she knew instinctively what she must do. She closed up her market stall, went home and packed a few things, and headed off towards Capernaum. She needed to find the healer. She had no more money left for any other doctors. Jesus was her only hope.

As she trudged along, Mara began thinking about her last time in Capernaum; and wondering about the possibility of seeing her daughter by chance of God's providence. She began imagining what her daughter might look like and what her adoptive parents had named her. It was only then that she came to realise that it was twelve years to the month, she had given birth to her baby girl. She began praying for a double miracle—to be healed of her bleeding issue and to see her daughter once more.

IF ONLY…
I CAN…

Upon arriving in Capernaum, Mara began asking everybody about where she could find this Yeshua of Nazareth. Many people shunned her, as they covered their nostrils from the stench; whilst others simply avoided her as they noticed her blood-stained clothing.

She was desperate to find her *Yeshua Moshia*". He was her only hope. She withdrew herself from the bustle of people and came across an isolated brook just outside of the city, where she was able to bathe herself as best she could and change her outer garments. No-one would suspect anything at least for a few hours. Feeling temporarily cleansed, she returned to the city streets and resumed her inquiries to find the teacher—the Healer—Jesus.

Eventually, she picked up on some clues she was hearing and began following a crowd of people towards the seashore. In no time she could see a movement of people coming her way. These excited people were surrounding one man. *"There he is!"* shouted someone in the crowd, and many raced to join the throng.

Mara moved quickly and cautiously as she purposefully forced her way through the crowd towards the Healer. However, she could not get near him as his disciples seemed to have formed a tight cordon around him. They passed her by but, as she turned to face the opposite direction, she was instantly swept along by the sheer force of people. It was at that moment she questioned the reality of forfeiting the opportunity to speak with Jesus in this situation. She had to find another way because the more energy she spent pushing through the crowd, the greater the risk that her bleeding symptoms would become once more evident.

Amid the momentum of the crowd, as bodies pushed and shoved, she felt as though she were being kneaded like bread dough. Then in a flash she saw a gap in the barrier of body guards. She said to herself "If I only I could reach out and touch the hem of his garment, I will be healed." She reached out her hand in desperation. "If only I can just touch the hem of his robe…" she repeated to herself. Using every ounce of energy she had, whilst holding her breath, blindly she stretched out her hand as far as she could reach. Then in an instant… the bleeding stopped. She experienced an electrifying power surge throughout her body. Right at that moment, she became acutely aware of the reality, she had been instantaneously healed of her terrible condition.

Suddenly, Jesus sensing that healing power had flowed from him, halted and turned around, scanning the crowd. He called out, "Who touched my robe? Who touched me?"

Over the noise of the crowd, his disciples called back to him, "Rabbi, look at this crowd pressing in on all sides! What are you talking about? How can you possibly ask, 'Who touched me?'"

But he kept on looking around to see who had intentionally touched his garment. Then Mara, frightened and trembling at the realization of what had just happened to her, came and fell to her knees in front of Jesus. She was a blubbering mess. He squatted down in front of her as she confessed what she had done. She so wanted to tell him the whole story, but in that instant—intuitively—somehow she could tell that he already knew. Jesus assisted her to her feet, looked directly at her and said, "Daughter of Abraham, your faith has made you well. Go in peace. *Noli respicere post tergum!* Your suffering is over. "

The teacher stood up, turned and moved on as quickly as he was able, whilst the disciples attempted to make headway through the crowd like an icebreaker through packed ice and snow.

Mara was left all alone. She was completely healed! She felt clean and fresh—inside and out. She was overcome with joy as the tears flowed. In that moment, she dropped to her knees again and raised her hands towards heaven in thankfulness and praise.

Ecstatically she began to process the reality of being healed after all these years. It restored her faith for a better future knowing that as she continued to seek the Lord with her whole heart, her mind, and her strength, *His will would unfold for her… in His way… in His time.*

Having received her physical healing, there was still one thing burning within her heart that she had so desperately longed for over the past twelve years: to see her daughter once more.

The throng moved on around her like water swishing past a huge boulder in the stream, as people continued pressing on to follow the teacher towards Jairus' house.

A short time later, one of Jairus' household servants arrived after pushing his way through the approaching crowd. Breathlessly, he reached Jairus with this message. "Sir, your daughter is dead. It's no use bothering the Teacher with this anymore."

Jairus was in shock. But before he could speak, Jesus reassuringly declared, " Stay calm Jairus. Don't be anxious or afraid my friend! Just believe. Hold onto your faith… and believe your daughter will be well again. She's going to be okay." The disciples continued to shield Jesus and Jairus moving at a steady pace—slowly working their way through the crowd.

As they approached the house, it appeared as if the whole neighbourhood were out the front in the street, accompanied by a full-on, woeful sound of mourning—weeping, wailing, loud crying.

Jesus firmly pronounced, "Please stop your weeping and wailing. The girl isn't dead as you think… she's actually only asleep!"

The mourners—some of whom would have been professional mourners—suddenly fell silent. Their woeful noise choked… into hushed silence. They knew for certain that the girl was dead, but their sudden silence became interrupted by a mixture of mocking and laughter as they scoffed at Jesus' comments. Others simply wondered what he actually meant by saying 'the girl was asleep.'

Jesus instructed everyone, including his disciples, to remain outside—everyone, that is, except for Simon, John, and James, and, of course, Jairus and his wife.

Jairus and his wife, Eunice led Jesus into the room where the girl's body lay. Taking the girl's hand Jesus asked Eunice what her daughter's name was.

Jesus spoke her name quietly in a loving tone. *"Tahlia! Tahlia!"*, as if he were gently trying to wake her from an afternoon nap. Then in a louder voice laced with such authority, he said, *"Tahlia! Child, get up!"* Immediately she started breathing again as her spirit returned. She opened her eyes and looked around to see her parents weeping for joy. Then she smiled as she sat up on the bed and looked straight into the welcoming, smiling face of Jesus.

Her parents were amazed and euphoric. They embraced her and showered her with hugs and kisses.

To help bring them back to some sense of reality, Jesus told them to give her something to eat. Then, before leaving he sternly instructed them to keep what had happened a secret. "Don't tell a soul what just occurred in this room."

However, as so often transpired following a number of Jesus' miracles, news quickly spread—like that of cooking odours wafting through an open kitchen window.

Jesus left the house and returned to Simon's place just three doors down the street, followed by the twelve disciples. Simon's house had become their headquarters for private gatherings and served as Jesus' home when they were not travelling.

It was in the privacy of this time and place that he gave them specific instructions about going out on a very special mission trip—without him. He commissioned them to preach the news of God's kingdom and heal the sick. In doing so he gave them his authority and power to deal with all the demons and cure diseases. He said, "Don't load yourselves up with a whole lot of travelling gear—no walking stick, no travel bag, no bread, no money, and don't take two shirts.

"Keep things as simple as possible; for all you need is yourselves and my authority. And don't look to be accommodated in comfort—accept whatever modest place you are invited to stay, and be content there until you leave. If you're not welcomed in a certain village, then leave that place. Don't make a scene. Simply shrug your shoulders, shake the dust from off your feet and move on."

Jesus prayed a blessing of shalom and protection over them. Each of the disciples then gathered up the provisions prepared for them by Simon's wife for the first part of their journey.

Commissioned by their Rabbi and filled with trepidation—yet empowered by his authority—they departed in various directions like sparks flying from a campfire. The disciples travelled in pairs, as each companion had been assigned by their Teacher. They quickly moved out from their home base, needing to reach their first destination before sunset, since the next day was Shabbat.

During their mission they moved from village to village, sharing the latest news of God—the message of hope found in Jesus—and healing people everywhere they went in His name.

While the disciples were away for a couple of weeks on their mission, Jesus withdrew from his public ministry to a secluded place for prayer and preparation for the next phase of his mission.

CB

CHAPTER TWELVE

TRUST IN THE LORD

The following day was Shabbat, and Mara planned to attend the synagogue before heading back home to Jerusalem. Not wanting to draw any attention to herself, she stood quite away from the entrance and waited as people were entering. Her eyes caught sight of a middle-aged woman and a beautiful auburn-haired girl with long, flowing curls that extended from under her head covering. She looked about twelve years old. It had to be her daughter. With her heart pounding heavily, she wondered could she gain a closer look without creating a scene?

Once the last person had entered the building, she walked towards the entrance, entered the building and stood at the back beside one of the columns—strategically positioning herself in order to be able to see the girl.

Jairus stood before the congregation to pray and read from the scriptures. In his prayer he acknowledged Adonai's faithfulness in all things… *'and especially for the miraculous raising of his daughter Tahlia from death.'*

By this time, everyone in the city knew how Jesus had come to the synagogue ruler's house the day before and healed his daughter. But in that moment—at the mention of Tahlia's name—Mara gasped. "Uh! Oh!" she whispered breathlessly, just loud enough to be heard by those nearby.

Even more strangely, Tahlia felt a quiver in her spirit. It was as if, even after twelve years of separation, she instinctively recognised her birth mother's sighing breath. Quickly she turned around to search in the direction of the gasp, just as the place erupted into spontaneous applause. Her mother, Eunice, also turned to acknowledge the applause.

In that very moment, Mara saw both their faces for the first time. Once again, she gasped.

The beautiful girl looked so much like Mara had, at that age; and Eunice her mother's face was radiant with joy and peace. For the briefest of moments, Taliah's wandering eyes were somehow drawn magnetically to Mara's face shining like the sun. She turned back to whisper something to her mother about this unusual experience. Eunice wrapped her arm around her with tenderness.

As the applause slowly dissipated and the congregation regained their attention, Jairus opened the parchment scroll and read from the book of Proverbs. Saying, "King Solomon wrote: '*Trust in the Lord with all your heart. Do not lean on your own understanding. In all your ways acknowledge him, and he will direct your paths.*'"

These words resonated like never before—as if they were electrified—especially for Mara, Eunice, Tahlia and Jairus. There was something quite mystical happening in that moment… as if Heaven had opened just wide enough to hear Adonai's voice of reassurance and approval. Jairus looked over at his wife and daughter. Eunice and Tahlia turned around simultaneously to catch sight of the woman at the back who had gasped so surprisingly moments earlier. Jairus, his wife, and daughter intuitively knew that this woman had been the answer to their prayers.

Mara wept tears of joy as she gazed at the three faces involved in this double miracle… knowing that only she and they knew what this particular scripture reading meant for each of them at this God-appointed time.

Eunice and Tahlia turned back towards Jairus to see that he also had tears of fulfilment and joy running down his beard. As they turned once more towards where Mara had been standing, they noticed that she had disappeared from sight. Where had she gone? Who was this stranger? What had brought her here on this day?

Mara had moved swiftly out of the synagogue. She raced as fast she could through the city streets and headed for home. Her heart was beating faster and faster as she ran… but even more so, her heart was bursting with thankfulness and joy. She was filled with contentment.

FIXATED ON MIRACLES

A few weeks after these two miracles, out on the grassy knoll not far from Bethsaida, the crowds had gathered from every direction. There must have been thousands of people. As they approached en masse toward the Teacher's small group, Jesus stood up in the middle of His disciples and looked around.

Even from a distance, the radiance of His face shone in the midday sun. Jesus had such compassion for the people, and with arms outstretched, he welcomed them and motioned for them to sit down.

Parents with children hustled for places near the front whilst older people, who were hard of hearing, also jostled for spots closer in order to hear the Teacher.

As the last of the multitude caught up and were seated, Jesus' disciples positioned themselves strategically throughout the centre as well as around the fringes of the large gathering. They enacted this routine after having rehearsed it a dozen times.

Jesus began to address the multitude, speaking loudly and clearly as he taught. He communicated about the Kingdom of God by using parables and stories of everyday things like seeds, weeds, trees and sheep. The people listened intently as Jesus mixed his teaching stories with some humorous analogies. For example: "Imagine a man trying to remove a tiny speck from his friend's eye while he's got a whole plank stuck in his own! He keeps bumping into everything, but he doesn't see the problem. In the same way, how can you point out others' faults when you've got bigger issues of your own to deal with?"

As the message was relayed all over the gathering, much laughter could be heard moving throughout like a wind coming off the lake and blowing through the trees.

Yosef and Asher had prime positions for seeing and hearing everything Jesus said and did. As the Teacher voiced His message, he would express his thoughts in a few phrases, then pause. What followed was a series of echoes, during which the disciples relayed the same messages along the chain of their strategic positions throughout the vast gathering. This way, every person—young and old—was able to hear the same message—from the first to the last, from the front to the back, and from one side to the other.

The crowd remained motionless and totally transfixed as they listened to the Teacher. After a while Yosef turned around and began to scan the crowd of profiled faces, clothing and hair colours. Some faces were vaguely familiar, but the majority were just faces. Then he saw them—his Uncle Jairus and his cousin Tahlia, whom Jesus had miraculously brought back to life a few weeks earlier. He tried to catch their attention by waving inconspicuously—but they too were totally focussed on the Teacher. He gave up and regained his attention on what the Teacher was saying.

As the day unfolded and the teaching completed, Jesus indicated to his disciples to allow those who wanted healing to approach. The disciples were fairly orderly in how they organised these desperate ones in need of 'a touch'. They knew from experience that it could become quite chaotic if they did not maintain some sort of order. As the people came for 'their touch or word', Jesus healed anyone who had need of healing: the blind, the lame, the crippled, the deaf, the mute, even the sick whose sickness was not visible, as well as the mentally deranged and demoniacs.

Yosef kept a keen eye on Jesus as He performed miracle after miracle. The young boy was fascinated as he watched the reactions of those who received their healing. Some jumped for joy, some wept, some raised their arms in gratitude and praise to Adonai, some yelled at the top of their lungs, and some simply fell at Jesus' feet, while others went away singing and rejoicing. A few others spontaneously hugged anyone who happened to be standing nearby.

CB

CHAPTER FOURTEEN

ADDING
AND
MULTIPLYING

As the afternoon wore on, Yosef also noticed that Jesus showed signs of weariness, even though he continued his healing ministry until the last person had received their blessing. The Teacher was looking exhausted after having spoken to the crowd for more than an hour, and then for another three hours, he had given of himself one-on-one to literally hundreds of people—from babies to children to the elderly.

Fortunately, Yosef was close enough to decipher the conversation between the disciples and Jesus. "It's getting late Master… you need to dismiss the people. Send them home or at least into the nearby villages for rest and food. Besides, Rabbi, you need some rest and nourishment yourself."

Whilst Yosef was not able to make out which of the disciples were actually speaking, at least he could understand what was being said.

It was then that Jesus turned directly to one particular disciple. "Philip, I'm thinking *we* should feed them before they start heading off but, as a local lad yourself, where do you think we could get enough food for such a large number of people? What are *your* thoughts?"

In his young mind, Yosef figured that Jesus possibly asked Philip not just because he was a local, but more than likely it was to test Philip's faith—well that's how it appeared to him, anyway.

Philip was very quick to reply. "Teacher, even if we could buy two hundred denarii worth of bread, it still wouldn't be near enough to feed everyone here! Surely each one would receive just a tiny morsal—not enough to satisfy!"

Yosef, having been so acutely tuned into their conversation, turned around to say something to Asher about his idea. However, his friend had wandered off, probably to speak with someone he knew or to stretch his legs before heading home.

It was getting late in the afternoon and Yosef was stirred within his heart and mind. He sprang into action. He had to speak to one of the disciples. He felt so insignificant as he worked his way towards where some of the disciples were standing. He tugged on the cloak of the one who looked like the main guy. Up close, this larger-than-life man turned around quickly, as if he were a guard on duty, and peered down at Yosef.

With a sense of urgency in his voice, Yosef politely pleaded with the man, "Excuse me sir, I need to speak to the Teacher and…"

The disciple abruptly interrupted him, "Go away boy! The Master has other things to deal with right now!"

"I know sir, that's why…" Yosef responded, but again the disciple interjected. "I said, not now! Go away!"

Just then another disciple, who looked younger and kinder, came and put his hand on the first disciple's shoulder. "It's okay Simon, I'll take care of this young lad." Simon grunted as he moved away, leaving Yosef with his rescuer.

To Yosef's astonishment, the second man squatted down to eyeball him. In a cheerful voice he said, "Oh, never mind my brother Simon… he's a bit like that with everyone! My name is Andrew… what's yours? And where might your Abba or Eema be… young fellow?"

Yosef introduced himself and explained that his father had been a fisherman who had sadly drowned. Andrew's heart was touched, and, having been a local fisherman himself, he told Yosef that he had known his Abba. "His name was Jared, right?" Yosef nodded.

Then Andrew asked, "Now, Yosef bar Jared, what is it you wanted to see the Teacher about that is so urgent, hey?"

"Please, Mr Andrew, would you give these to the Teacher to feed the people? I believe he will know what to do and how to do it. Please?!"

Andrew leaned forward with a broad smile and placed his hand on Yosef's shoulder. Then looking into the knapsack, he saw five small loaves of bread and two small fish. "The Lord bless you son. Yes, I'm sure the Teacher will be most appreciative of your contribution. You can come with me and give it to Jesus yourself! Come this way."

Making his way through the people, who were already becoming restless and standing, Andrew led Yosef towards the Teacher. Yosef stood back a bit whilst Andrew spoke quietly to Jesus. The Teacher replied just loud enough for Yosef to hear, "Bring the boy here!"

Andrew motioned for Yosef to approach. Jesus turned and knelt on one knee and asked his name. Yosef replied. "My name is Yosef, Teacher."

"Yosef… hmm? Oh yes, I saw you up in that sycamore tree! That was a really great idea!" Jesus said, winking at him.

"Yosef… hey? What a wonderful name. My Abba's name was Yosef too! Do you know what your name means, son?" Jesus spoke ever so gently—his voice sounded even kinder than when he spoke to the crowds.

"Yes sir. It means *'God adds'*… I think!"

Nodding, Jesus replied, "You are absolutely right, young Yosef! Now tell me, do you also happen to know what we call it when we take the same thing and add it over and over again?"

Yosef answered keenly, "Oh yes, sir, I believe it is called multiply… or something like that!"

Jesus gave him a fist bump. "Right again, my little friend of faith." Leaning in closer, Jesus lowered his voice. "Do you also happen to know the name we use to describe the 'One Who is more than enough'?"

"Is it El Shaddai?"

"Excellent!" Jesus replied. "Okay, Yosef, brace yourself, for you are about to see El Shaddai do some very rapid adding and multiplying… and it will be '*more than enough!*' Are you ready?"

"Oh yes sir!" Yosef exclaimed. "I believe that you can do much more with this small amount… much, much more than I could dream of or imagine!"

Jesus placed his hand on Yosef's head and blessed him. Standing upright he took the knapsack and said, "Thank you for your kindness and faith."

Turning immediately towards Andrew who had witnessed this intimate encounter, Jesus asked him, "How many did you say, Andrew?"

"I believe we have five loaves and two fish, Rabbi," Andrew replied.

Jesus motioned to Simon to call all the disciples together. The instructions Jesus gave them were simple and clear. "Quickly move amongst the people before they begin to leave. Tell them to sit down again, but this time organize them into groups of fifties or hundreds."

Once again, it felt as if time had slowed down for Yosef as he stood there, watching the disciples move swiftly and smoothly through the multitude. He was fascinated to see such a large number of people regroup and sit down again, like leaves swirling together in a gentle breeze, finding their place on the ground.

Asher suddenly reappeared on the scene as if from out of nowhere. He'd snuck up behind Yosef yammering, "Hey Yoyo, what's happening?" Once again Yosef was startled and jumped around declaring, "Asher don't' do that!" Then once his racing heart began to slow down, he took a couple of deep breaths and explained to his friend about his encounter with Jesus. "Ash, get yourself ready... 'cos I think we about to see the *biggest* miracle of all!"

CHAPTER FIFTEEN

THE BIGGEST MIRACLE

Just as the boys sat down, Jairus and Tahlia found them and joined their group of fifty. This was such a wonderful experience to share with his Dohd Jairus, his Dodan Tahlia and, of course, his best chaver—Asher. Jairus questioned the children about what they'd understood from the Teacher's message.

What had been their favourite story?... and which parts they would like to know more about?

Yosef was bursting to tell his uncle and cousin about his meeting with Jesus. "Uncle, I believe that the Teacher is going to do another miracle. This one will be a miracle of multiplication!"

In the meantime, as the disciples moved about the multitude, organising them into groups of fifties and hundreds, Jesus mysteriously had found twelve baskets. Then, once Jesus had received the relayed message that everyone was settled in their groups, he called the disciples back.

A mystifying hush of expectancy once again swept over the crowd—almost as if everyone were simultaneously holding their breath. Jesus took up his position, and taking Yosef's offering of the five small loaves of bread, he held them out as he lifted his face toward heaven in prayer. Jesus prayed so softly that not even Yosef, with his acute hearing, could interpret what he was saying. Then he did the same with the two fish.

Amongst the vast crowd, there was neither a movement nor a sound, as they were completely absorbed in what was happening. Nobody in the assembly had any idea of what was about to unfold before their eyes—except for Jesus and Yosef, who was beside himself with wonder and anticipation.

After the prayer of thanksgiving, Jesus began methodically breaking the bread and the fish into Andrews' basket first. Andrew set out to distribute what he had been given. Then Jesus did the same for Simon, then James, then John, then Philip and so on until all the disciples moved amongst the multitude.

Yosef was amazed, firstly at the miracle of seeing Jesus breaking the bread and fish into pieces until all the baskets were full. He was witnessing firsthand a miracle of *adding and multiplying* just as Jesus had told him. Somehow, Jesus just kept on adding to each of the disciples' baskets until they were full. Not only had Yosef's small food offering been multiplied masterfully by Jesus' handiwork, but it had been multiplied twelve times!

But that's not all! As the miracle of multiplication continued with the disciples moving throughout the throng of people in their numbered groups, a waft of freshly baked bread swept over the crowd. Standing on his tiptoes, Yosef continued to watch as far as his eyes could see in every direction. In fact, Asher later told Yosef how he'd seen his eyes grow bigger and bigger like saucers as he witnessed this miracle unfolding.

Each of the disciples moved from group to group, distributing the morsels of bread and fish. It appeared that everyone… every man, woman and child—just kept taking food from the baskets as they came past. Everyone ate to their hearts' content!

It seemed that every person had lost all concept of time as this miracle was taking place; as they had also lost their focus on Jesus. In a sudden flash of time-awareness, Yosef turned around to look for Jesus, but where was he? He was nowhere to be seen! Had he slipped off into the background and disappeared, exhausted?

Yosef scanned dozens of groups sitting and eating... then he found him. There was Jesus, seated among a group mostly consisting of women and children. He too was snacking on some morsels of this miraculous food himself. In that fleeting moment, Jesus turned to see Yosef looking at him. The Teacher smiled and mouthed, "*Thank you*," as he once again winked at the young boy of faith. After that, Yosef noticed Jesus move on to engage with another group, then another, and another.

Eventually the disciples and Jesus regrouped near where they had started from earlier. The disciples reported that everyone had eaten, but then it appeared that Jesus insisted his friends should also sit down and eat—which they did. Their baskets were now empty… but the miracle was not quite finished!

After several minutes, Jesus instructed them to move throughout the assembly of people one last time and collect any leftovers. As they shuffled about gathering the scraps, the people also began standing ready for moving on. About this time, Jesus stood up with his hands raised and signalled to them that they were dismissed and free to return to their homes. He blessed them with his 'Shalom' in every direction.

From that point the crowd gradually began to dwindle as the last of the baskets were collected. Yosef's group was one of the last to leave. Uncle Jairus told the three children that it was time to leave so that they could be home before dark. As they turned to go, Yosef screamed out, "Uncle Jairus! *Wait please*! My knapsack!"

No sooner had he said that and turned around to retrieve his empty knapsack, there was the disciple Andrew standing right there. "Here you go young Yosef. I believe this is yours! Thank you for your generosity and faith my friend."

As Andrew handed the knapsack to Yosef, the boy had a strong impression that yet another miracle had occurred. Yosef received what appeared to be—and what he expected to be—an empty, lightweight bag. Yet, as he took it from Andrew, he noticed that it was heavy and full! He looked at his uncle, his cousin, his chaver, and then finally at Andrew in puzzlement.

With a broad smile, Andrew explained, "The Teacher didn't want you to go home empty-handed. This is for you to share with your Eema and Sarta." Yosef's heart was full of joy and amazement. "Thank you, Andrew. And yes, I will tell them all about this wonderful miracle story."

"Oh, and one more thing," Andrew added. "The Teacher asked me to remind you that what looks impossible to people… is possible with God! Continue to trust Adonai and He will give you the increase." They fist bumped, and then Andrew left.

No sooner had Andrew left than another man appeared before the small group. This time it was Andrew's brother Simon—the big, burly disciple who had told him to go away. Squatting down to Yosef's level and using a much friendlier tone of voice, he said, "Thanks, little guy… Yosef, isn't it?" Yosef nodded. "I'm sorry for the way I spoke to you earlier. It seems that I've still got a lot to learn, hey?

"I am so glad that my brother Andrew spotted you. Yosef don't ever let anyone put you down because of your age. Your faith was much bigger than mine today! Shalom." And with that Simon went to rejoin his friends.

ര

CHAPTER SIXTEEN

LET THE BOY SPEAK

Yosef and Asher, as well as his Dohd and Dodan, were among one of the last of the groups to leave the grassy knoll. They needed to move quickly as it was getting rather late. Along the way the two boys and Tahlia talked about everything they had seen and heard during the day.

Their group stuck to the main track all the way to Capernaum. Asher and Yosef bid farewell to Jairus and Tahlia, wearily continuing along with the dwindling group of pilgrims on their journey home. For safety reasons, this time the boys did not deviate from the main route, as the sun slowly began to disappear behind the hills.

Eventually the boys separated from each other as they reached Asher's home first. Yosef ran to keep up with the small group of people walking towards his village. Upon his arrival at home, there was his Eema waiting in the doorway… looking very stern-faced… standing with hands on hips! "Yosef bar Jared, where have you been? I've been worried sick about you all afternoon!

"You will need to have a pretty convincing story of where and why you've been… or… or… I'll have no choice but to ground you from spending time with Asher for at least a week! Now, young man, what do you have to say for yourself? Hmm?!" his mother demanded.

Then, without so much as taking a breath, just as she was about to continue her ranting, her own Eema interjected. "Oh, let the boy speak Miriam! You know the boys went to hear the Teacher. I'm sure he has a really good explanation if you'll just let him speak!"

Yosef was surprised to hear his Sarta speak that way. He had never heard her speak that way—ever. He felt embarrassed for his Eema but, at the same time, it actually gave him courage to speak.

Right at that very moment, as he opened his mouth to begin his explanation, there was a knock at the door. By this time the sun had set and cautiously Miriam opened the door just a fraction to see who was there. Then she opened the door wide and in came Jairus and Tahlia, and behind them, looking rather sheepish, was Asher.

"Shalom, Miriam and Abigail," Jairus greeted as he approached the two women and kissed them fondly. Tahlia also greeted her Dodah (Auntie) and Sarta. He continued, "Your sister, Eunice, and her Shvigger (mother-in-law), Sarah, send their greetings to you both."

Jairus apologised for the unexpected visit and being so late. He went on to explain how the boys had walked back to his home along with a group of fellow pilgrims, and how he'd farewelled the boys on their way to their own homes. But when he went inside his house, his strong-willed wife, Eunice, had insisted that he and Tahlia follow the boys as quickly as possible to make sure they arrived home safely. "We kept our distance far enough back so that they were not aware we there behind them."

Jairus respectfully explained, "Once the boys had separated, we quickly called into Asher's home and asked if he could accompany us to your house." He went on to clarify further, "Miriam, your sister Eunice, knew that you would be very concerned about Yosef. She insisted that we not only ensure he arrived home safely, but also that we should be here to support him. She knew that he would no doubt receive a grilling of scolding words and would be required to give an account of where he'd been and why he was home so late."

Miriam was somewhat taken aback, but graciously expressed her appreciation for their concern. "Actually, Yosef was just about to explain his whereabouts when you arrived!" she said with a slight hint of cynical accusation in her voice. "Weren't you son?"

"Yes, Eema," Yosef replied. "And thank you Uncle Jairus for your kind thoughtfulness and help," he began rather tentatively. He took a deep breath and excitedly went on to convey his story from beginning to end. He shared about how he and Asher had taken the short cut, only to arrive and see Jesus and his disciples getting into the boats and heading for Bethsaida. He spoke of what it was like being part of such a huge crowd of people, listening to the Teacher's stories and then seeing people healed.

He paused as he looked at his cousin Tahlia, who was smiling, and his friend Asher, who was listening intently and reliving their adventurous day. After taking a deep breath, he continued, explaining in even more detail about his encounter with Andrew, Simon, and Jesus. *"He took my lunch, Eema!"* Yosef declared with joy and amazement. He was almost beside himself as he spoke about seeing his knapsack of food being broken and distributed to feed all the people. He paused again, realizing that his Sarta and Eema had tears running down their cheeks.

He explained about the leftovers being collected and receiving the Teacher's blessing through Andrew, as well as Simon's apology. At this point, he picked up the knapsack from the floor and handed it to his Eema. She spilled the contents onto the table, and there before them was a spread of bread and fish that was far more than what she had given to Yosef earlier in the day!

"Eema, Andrew was a fisherman just like Abba, and he said that he had known him!" exclaimed Yosef. "He told me that the Teacher had asked me to share this food with you and Sarta, and that the Teacher wanted us to remember… nothing is impossible with God, and that Adonai will always provide the increase… just like my name means."

Wiping the tears from her face with her apron, Yosef's Eema came over and hugged him tightly. "Yosef, I'm sorry for doubting you, my son.

Your Abba would be very proud of you for sharing your lunch, as am I, and having the 'faith of a mustard seed' as the Teacher says. Adonai has certainly blessed you with the gift of great faith, my son." And with that everyone in the room, shouted "Amen!"

Jairus cleared his throat, and spoke again. "And, Yosef, we too are thrilled that you have indeed experienced your own miracle today. For your Dodan and I to have Jesus raise our daughter back to life is a miracle for sure. But to see a young boy's lunch—*your* lunch—feed more than five thousand people… now that is something else!" He stepped closer to Yosef and placed his hand on his head, "And somehow, young man, I have a strange feeling, that this miracle of the five loaves and two fishes was made possible because of your faith. And I also believe there is more to come! Yosef, I believe that Adonai will continue a ministry of multiplication through you… to bless others."

At this, Jairus led them in a prayer of thanksgiving for God's protection and provision. Then they all sat down and broke bread together. The little house was filled with much laughter and even more stories.

CB

Faith grows as Yosef's Story continues ...

From that day, Yosef began helping his Eema and Sarta bake loaves of bread which they not only sold, but also gave away to anyone who could not afford to pay. Every week Yosef and Asher would venture out travelling up to Capernaum on their own mission distributing bread to the beggars on the streets.

In Miriam's household, they always had enough oil and flour, as long as they kept giving bread away and sharing the good news about Jesus.

In time, Yosef became a fisherman just like his Abba but more importantly, he learned to follow in the footsteps of Jesus, who had called Simon, Andrew, James and John to be fishers of men.

Every time Yosef set out to fish, it seemed that he was accompanied by an invisible blessing. As he cast his net into the shimmering waters, he often found himself reeling in an abundance of fish—more than any of the other fishermen on the shore. While others returned with their modest catches, Yosef's boat brimmed with glistening silvers and golden scales, sparkling like jewels in the morning sun. And every day, it seemed he was able to give away more than what he had caught.

Yosef eagerly continued to take every opportunity to tell others about how Jesus had taken his lunch. Every day he would declare in faith: *"Yeah! And He still multiplies my tiny offering of faith. He is still taking my lunch!"*

To those who listened, Yosef would always leave them with this challenge:

"What do you have in your hands? Offer it up to El Shaddai in faith… and watch what He does with it! After all… He is the God Who is more than enough!"

ᘓ

Faith grows as Tahlia's Story continues …

Over a period of years, Jairus took young Asher under his wing and trained him in all matters concerning the synagogue—from administration and record keeping ,to caring for the sanctuary and sacred articles, as well as the Shabbat proceedings.

Many years later, Jairus and the elders unanimously agreed to bestow upon Asher the daily responsibilities of running the synagogue.

Tahlia continued to be in good health as she grew into a beautiful woman. She and Asher grew closer in their friendship and betrothed themselves to each other.

After they were married and began to raise their own family, Tahlia's heart was moved towards helping children in need of care. She became known throughout the district as the girl whom Jesus had brought back to life with his command, '*Little girl, get up!*' But she was also recognized for her work in rescuing children and giving them new life and hope in times of need.

Asher and Tahlia became influential leaders within the community of Jesus' followers in Capernaum during the early years of the church.

Tahlia took every opportunity to share her story of healing—being raised from the dead. She passionately exercised a powerful healing ministry among women and children, especially babies.

CB

Faith grows as Mara's Story continues …

Mara returned to her grandparents' home in Jerusalem, where she had been raised, and reestablished her grandfather's baking business. Operating her market stall with much joy and exuberance, she would take every opportunity to share her story of faith and healing while willingly praying for anyone in need.

Over time, she discovered that the Lord had given her a deep compassion for young teenage girls and so, she became a mentor to hundreds over the years. She taught them the phrase: '*Noli respicere post tergum*', and how to apply the principle of '*do not look back*' to their lives.

Eventually, Mara married and had children of her own. She and her husband became strong Christian witnesses and were very active in the church in Jerusalem.

As this story draws to a close, you may be wondering about Dimitrius. Did he become a Christian after being one of the Roman soldiers involved in the crucifixion of Jesus? Did he eventually return to seek out his first love?

The author will now leave you to speculate with two final burning questions:

Who did Mara marry, and what motivated her decision?

GLOSSARY
of
HEBREW TERMS

Dohd: *Uncle*

Dodan: *Cousin*

Dodah: *Aunty*

Chaver: *Friend*

Eema: *Mother*

Abba: *Father*

Savta: *Grandmother*

Shvigger: *Mother-in-law*

Shabbat: *Sabbath*

Yosef bar Jared: *Yosef son of Jared*

Shiva: *Funeral*

Adonai: *LORD*

Shloshim: *30 days of mourning*

Yeshua Moshia': *Jesus the Saviour*

Denarii: *one day's wage for labour*

El Shaddai: *The All-Sufficient One / The God Who is more than enough.*

OTHER BOOKS
by
Gary Lewis

VERTICALLY CHALLENGED* - The Ups and Downs of Praying [adults/teens]

PRAYER BUBBLES* - Turning Thoughts into Prayers for Prayer Hesitants [adults/teens]

AN EPISTLE TO AN APOSTLE* - Titus writes to Paul (a novella Bible story) [adults/teens]

LITTLE BOY ALL LOCKED UP* (a novella about anger, grief & loss) [all ages]

STOLEN TRUTH AND THE DARK-HOODED THIEF* (a novella about lying & stealing) [all ages]

JESSICA FINDS TRUE VALUE (a picture story book about self-worth)

JACKSON'S HIDDEN TREASURE (a picture story book about self-worth)

OLIVIA'S JAR OF PICKLED INSPIRATION (a picture story book about positive affirmation)

*** specific Christian content**

www.gablesbooks.com

ABOUT the AUTHOR

Gary Lewis is a retired Primary School Chaplain and mentor to School Chaplains. His background has involved Primary School education, Children's Ministry including Church Pastor. His extensive lay ministry covering more than 50 years, has also involved Worship Leading, Preaching, Prayer Ministry Coordinator and Church leadership.

He has been married to Maree for 50 years, with 3 children and 7 grandchildren. In his retirement, Gary continues mentoring in various capacities, as well as running several workshops in different fields… including prayer, discipleship, writing and storytelling.